Praise for Richard Herman's previous novels

'This is the sharp end, with vivid descriptions of air combat, the smell of hot oil and fear' – *The Times*

'Truly edge of the seat exciting' – Dale Brown

'Could very well be tomorrow's headlines' – Clive Cussler

'"Thinking man's" thrillers that out-Clancy Clancy' – *Kirkus*

'A powerful picture of global politics and military tactical action, with his mastery of the air evident in every pulsating page' – *Oxford Times*

About the Author

Richard Herman is a former combat pilot who has flown over 200 missions himself. He was stationed in Vietnam, West Germany and Great Britain. He has flown the F-4 and the C-130 and received five medals, including the Bronze Star. He retired from the US Air Force in 1983 with the rank of Major after serving for twenty-one years. He has since written nine previous highly acclaimed thrillers: *The Warbirds, Force of Eagles, Firebreak, Mosquito Run, Dark Wing, Iron Gate, The Power Curve, Against All Enemies* and *Edge of Honour*. He and his English-born wife now live in Gold River, California.

The Trojan Sea

Richard Herman

CORONET BOOKS

Hodder & Stoughton

First published in Great Britain in 2001
by Hodder and Stoughton
First published in paperback in 2001
by Hodder and Stoughton
A division of Hodder Headline

A Coronet Paperback

10 9 8 7 6 5 4 3 2 1

A CIP catalogue record for this title is available
from the British Library

ISBN 0 340 73828 6

Printed and bound in Great Britain by
Mackays of Chatham plc, Chatham, Kent

Hodder and Stoughton
A division of Hodder Headline
338 Euston Road
London NW1 3BH

For Sheila,
who made all this possible

Acknowledgements

While this novel is a work of fiction, I tried to base it in reality. In it I went far beyond my own area of expertise and am indebted to those who shared their experiences and knowledge. Mike Curtis spent hours introducing me to the complex and fascinating world of oil, while Perry Fisher, *World Oil* magazine, was willing to take the time to answer a host of questions from a complete stranger and provide invaluable leads.

Brian Carroll, who logged nearly three thousand hours flying Lightnings – first for the RAF, where he served as the Chief Flight Examiner Strike Command (Fighters), and later as Chief Flying Instructor Royal Saudi Air Force – spent a weekend captivating me with the saga of the Lightning. He then had to spend countless hours tutoring me in the details. And while I was a poor student, I enjoyed every minute.

A word about the Lightning. A total of 337 Lightnings were built by English Electric, now known as British Aerospace, and served in the RAF from 1960 to 1987. They were also flown by the Kuwaiti and Royal Saudi Air Force. The Lightning was unique and a classic fighter, and the only supersonic jet built by Britain on its own. Designed as a point defense fighter, it exceeded all expectations in its superb performance, and its initial rate of climb of fifty-thousand feet per minute was breathtaking. It is a pilot's airplane in every respect, and it was a sad day when they were finally phased out of service.

Jeff Ackland of Performance Aircraft was kind enough to allow me to write about the Legend, and his aircraft does perform as described. Dr Richard Hawkins made the Sabreliner come alive and, in the process, made me deeply envious. At the Pentagon, Mr Robert Boyd intrigued me with the plans–intelligence interface, which is worth a story in itself,

Unnatural Causes

P. D. JAMES

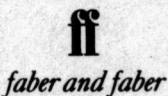

faber and faber

First published in 1967
by Faber and Faber Limited
3 Queen Square London WC1N 3AU
Published by Sphere Books in 1973
Published by Penguin Books in 1989
This paperback edition published by Faber and Faber in 2002

Photoset by RefineCatch Limited, Bungay, Suffolk
Printed in England by Mackays of Chatham plc, Chatham, Kent

All rights reserved

© P. D. James, 1967

A CIP record for this book
is available from the British Library

ISBN 0–571–20410–4

2 4 6 8 10 9 7 5 3 1

CONTENTS

BOOK ONE

CHAPTER ONE

The corpse without hands lay in the bottom of a small sailing dinghy drifting just within sight of the Suffolk coast. It was the body of a middle-aged man, a dapper little cadaver, its shroud a dark pin-striped suit which fitted the narrow body as elegantly in death as it had in life. The hand-made shoes still gleamed except for some scuffing of the toe caps, the silk tie was knotted under the prominent Adam's apple. He had dressed with careful orthodoxy for the town, this hapless voyager; not for this lonely sea; nor for this death.

It was early afternoon in mid-October and the glazed eyes were turned upwards to a sky of surprising blue across which the light south-west wind was dragging a few torn rags of cloud. The wooden shell, without mast or rowlocks, bounced gently on the surge of the North Sea so that the head shifted and rolled as if in restless sleep. It had been an unremarkable face even in life and death had given it nothing but a pitiful vacuity. The fair hair grew sparsely from a high bumpy forehead, the nose was so narrow that the white ridge of bone looked as if it were about to pierce the flesh; the mouth, small and thin-lipped, had dropped open to reveal two prominent front teeth which gave the whole face the supercilious look of a dead hare.

The legs, still clamped in rigor, were wedged one each side of the centre-board case and the forearms had been placed resting on the thwart. Both hands had been taken off at the wrists. There had been little bleeding. On each forearm a trickle of blood had spun a black web between the stiff fair hairs and the thwart was stained as if it had been used as a chopping block. But that was all; the rest of the body and the boards of the dinghy were free of blood.

3

The right hand had been taken cleanly off and the curved end of the radius glistened white; but the left had been bungled and the jagged splinters of bone, needle sharp, stuck out from the receding flesh. Both jacket sleeves and shirt cuffs had been pulled up for the butchery and a pair of gold initialled cuff links dangled free, glinting as they slowly turned and were caught by the autumn sun.

The dinghy, its paintwork faded and peeling, drifted like a discarded toy on an almost empty sea. On the horizon the divided silhouette of a coaster was making her way down the Yarmouth Lanes; nothing else was in sight. About two o'clock a black dot swooped across the sky towards the land trailing its feathered tail and the air was torn by the scream of engines. Then the roar faded and there was again no sound but the sucking of the water against the boat and the occasional cry of a gull.

Suddenly the dinghy rocked violently, then steadied itself and swung slowly round. As if sensing the strong tug of the on-shore current, it began to move more purposefully. A black-headed gull, which had dropped lightly on to the prow and had perched there, rigid as a figurehead, rose with wild cries to circle above the body. Slowly, inexorably, the water dancing at the prow, the little boat bore its dreadful cargo towards the shore.

CHAPTER TWO

Just before two o'clock on the afternoon of the same day Superintendent Adam Dalgliesh drove his Cooper Bristol gently on to the grass verge outside Blythburgh Church and, a minute later, passed through the north chantry-chapel door into the cold silvery whiteness of one of the loveliest church interiors in Suffolk. He was on his way to Monksmere Head just south of Dunwich to spend a ten-day autumn holiday with a spinster aunt, his only living relative, and this was his last stop on the

way. He had started off from his City flat before London was stirring, and instead of taking the direct route to Monksmere through Ipswich, had struck north at Chelmsford to enter Suffolk at Sudbury. He had breakfasted at Long Melford and had then turned west through Lavenham to drive slowly and at will through the green and gold of this most unspoilt and unprettified of counties. His mood would have wholly matched the day if it weren't for one persistent nagging worry. He had been deliberately putting off a personal decision until this holiday. Before he went back to London he must finally decide whether to ask Deborah Riscoe to marry him.

Irrationally, the decision would have been easier if he hadn't known so certainly what her answer would be. This threw upon him the whole responsibility for deciding whether to change the present satisfactory status quo (well, satisfactory for him anyway, and it could be argued surely that Deborah was happier now than she had been a year ago?) for a commitment which both of them, he suspected, would regard as irrevocable no matter what the outcome. There are few couples as unhappy as those who are too proud to admit their unhappiness. Some of the hazards he knew. He knew that she disliked and resented his job. This wasn't surprising nor, in itself, important. The job was his choice and he had never required anyone's approval or encouragement. But it was a daunting prospect that every late duty, every emergency, might have to be preceded by an apologetic telephone call. As he walked to and fro under the marvellous cambered tie-beam roof and smelt the Anglican odour of wax polish, flowers and damp old hymn books, it came to him that he had got what he wanted at almost the precise moment of suspecting that he no longer wanted it. This experience is too common to cause an intelligent man lasting disappointment but it still has power to disconcert. It wasn't the loss of freedom that deterred him; the men who squealed most about that were usually the least free. Much more difficult to face was the loss of privacy. Even the loss of physical privacy was hard to accept. Running his

fingers over the carved fifteenth-century lectern he tried to picture life in the Queenhithe flat with Deborah always there, no longer the eagerly awaited visitor but part of his life, the legal, certificated next of kin.

It had been a bad time at the Yard to be faced with personal problems. There had recently been a major reorganisation which had resulted in the inevitable disruption of loyalties and of routine, the expected crop of rumours and discontent. And there had been no relief from the pressure of work. Most of the senior officers were already working a fourteen-hour day. His last case, although successful, had been particularly tedious. A child had been murdered and the investigation had turned into a man hunt of the kind he most disliked and was temperamentally least suited for – a matter of dogged, persistent checking of facts carried on in a blaze of publicity and hindered by the fear and hysteria of the neighbourhood. The child's parents had fastened on him like drowning swimmers gulping for reassurance and hope and he could still feel the almost physical load of their sorrow and guilt. He had been required to be at once a comforter and father-confessor, avenger and judge. There was nothing new to him in this. He had felt no personal involvement in their grief, and this detachment had, as always, been his strength, as the anger and intense, outraged commitment of some of his colleagues, faced with the same crime, would have been theirs. But the strain of the case was still with him and it would take more than the winds of a Suffolk autumn to clean his mind of some images. No reasonable woman could have expected him to propose marriage in the middle of this investigation and Deborah had not done so. That he had found time and energy to finish his second book of verse a few days before the arrest was something which neither of them had mentioned. He had been appalled to recognise that even the exercise of a minor talent could be made the excuse for selfishness and inertia. He hadn't liked himself much recently, and it was perhaps sanguine to hope that this holiday could alter that.

6

Half an hour later he closed the church door quietly behind him and set off on the last few miles of the journey to Monksmere. He had written to his aunt to say that he would probably arrive at half-past two and, with luck, he would be there almost precisely on time. If, as was usual, his aunt came out of the cottage at two-thirty she should see the Cooper Bristol just breasting the headland. He thought of her tall, angular, waiting figure with affection. There was little unusual about her story and most of it he had guessed, picked up as a boy from snatches of his mother's unguarded talk or had simply known as one of the facts of his childhood. Her fiancé had been killed in 1918 just six months before the Armistice when she was a young girl. Her mother was a delicate, spoilt beauty, the worst possible wife for a scholarly country clergyman as she herself frequently admitted, apparently thinking that this candour both justified and excused in advance the next outbreak of selfishness or extravagance. She disliked the sight of other people's grief since it rendered them temporarily more interesting than herself and she decided to take young Captain Maskell's death very hard. Whatever her sensitive, uncommunicative and rather difficult daughter suffered it must be apparent that her mother suffered more; and three weeks after the telegram was received she died of influenza. It is doubtful whether she intended to go to such lengths but she would have been gratified by the result. Her distraught husband forgot in one night all the irritations and anxieties of his marriage and remembered only his wife's gaiety and beauty. It was, of course, unthinkable that he should marry again, and he never did. Jane Dalgliesh, whose own bereavement hardly anyone now had the time to remember, took her mother's place as hostess at the vicarage and remained with her father until his retirement in 1945 and his death ten years later. She was a highly intelligent woman and if she found unsatisfying the annual routine of housekeeping and parochial activities, predictable and inescapable as the liturgical year, she never said so. Her father was so assured of the ultimate importance of his

calling that it never occurred to him that anyone's gifts could be wasted in its service. Jane Dalgliesh, respected by the parishioners but never loved, did what had to be done and solaced herself with her study of birds. After her father's death the papers she published, records of meticulous observation, brought her some notice; and in time what the parish had patronisingly described as 'Miss Dalgliesh's little hobby' made her one of the most respected of amateur ornithologists. Just over five years ago she had sold her house in Lincolnshire and bought Pentlands, a stone cottage on the edge of Monksmere Head. Here Dalgliesh visited her at least twice a year.

They were no mere duty visits, although he would have felt a responsibility for her if she were not so obviously self-sufficient that, at times, even to feel affection seemed a kind of insult. But the affection was there and both of them knew it. Already he was looking forward to the satisfaction of seeing her, to the assured pleasures of a holiday at Monksmere.

There would be a driftwood fire in the wide hearth scenting the whole cottage, and before it the high-backed armchair once part of his father's study in the vicarage where he was born, the leather smelling of childhood. There would be a sparsely furnished bedroom with a view of sea and sky, a comfortable if narrow bed with sheets smelling faintly of wood-smoke and lavender, plenty of hot water and a bath long enough for a six-foot-two man to stretch himself in comfort. His aunt was herself six foot tall and had a masculine appreciation of essential comforts. More immediately, there would be tea before the fire and hot buttered toast with home-made potted meat. Best of all, there would be no corpses and no talk of them. He suspected that Jane Dalgliesh thought it odd that an intelligent man should choose to earn his living catching murderers and she was not a woman to feign polite interest when she felt none. She made no demands on him, not even the demands of affection, and because of this she was the only woman in the world with whom he was completely at peace. He knew exactly what the holiday offered. They would walk together,

8

often in silence, on the damp strip of firm sand between the sea's foam and the pebbled rises of the beach. He would carry her sketching paraphernalia, she would stride a little ahead, hands dug in her jacket pockets, eyes searching out where wheatears, scarcely distinguishable from pebbles, had lighted on the shingle, or following the flight of tern or plover. It would be peaceful, restful, utterly undemanding; but at the end of ten days he would go back to London with a sense of relief.

He was driving now through Dunwich Forest where the Forestry Commission's plantations of dark firs flanked the road. He fancied that he could smell the sea now, the salt tang borne to him on the wind was sharper than the bitter smell of the trees. His heart lifted. He felt like a child coming home. And now the forest ended, the sombre dark green of the firs ruled off by a wire fence from the water-coloured fields and hedges. And now they too passed and he was driving through the gorse and heather of the heathlands on his way to Dunwich. As he reached the village and turned right up the hill which skirted the walled enclosure of the ruined Franciscan friory there was the blare of a car's horn and a Jaguar, driven very fast, shot past. He glimpsed a dark head, and a hand raised in salute before, with a valedictory hoot, the car was out of sight. So Oliver Latham, the dramatic critic, was at his cottage for the weekend. That was hardly likely to inconvenience Dalgliesh for Latham did not come to Suffolk for company. Like his near neighbour, Justin Bryce, he used his cottage as a retreat from London, and perhaps from people, although he was at Monksmere less frequently than Bryce. Dalgliesh had met him once or twice and had recognised in him a restlessness and tension which found an echo in his own character. He was known to like fast cars and fast driving, and Dalgliesh suspected that it was in the drive to and from Monksmere that he found his release. It was difficult to imagine why else he kept on his cottage. He came to it seldom, never brought his women there, took no interest in furnishing it, and used it chiefly as a

9

base for wild drives around the district which were so violent and irrational that they seemed a kind of abreaction.

As Rosemary Cottage came into sight on the bend of the road Dalgliesh accelerated. He had little hope of driving past unobserved but at least he could drive at a speed which made it unreasonable to stop. As he shot past he just had time to see out of the corner of his eye a face at an upstairs window. Well, it was to be expected. Celia Calthrop regarded herself as the doyenne of the small community at Monksmere and had assigned herself certain duties and privileges. If her neighbours were so ill-advised as not to keep her informed of the comings and goings of themselves and their visitors she was prepared to take some trouble to find out for herself. She had a quick ear for an approaching car and the situation of her cottage, just where the rough track across the headland joined the road from Dunwich, gave her every opportunity of keeping an eye on things.

Miss Calthrop had bought Brodie's Barn, re-named Rosemary Cottage, twelve years previously. She had got it cheap and by gentle but persistent bullying of local labour, had converted it equally cheaply from a pleasing if shabby stone house to the romanticised ideal of her readers. It frequently featured in women's magazines as 'Celia Calthrop's delightful Suffolk residence where, amid the peace of the countryside, she creates those delightful romances which so thrill our readers'. Inside, Rosemary Cottage was very comfortable in its pretentious and tasteless way; outside, it had everything its owner considered appropriate to a country cottage, a thatched roof (deplorably expensive to insure and maintain), a herb garden (a sinister looking patch this; Miss Calthrop was not successful with herbs), a small artificial pond (malodorous in summer) and a dovecote (but doves obstinately refused to roost in it). There was also a sleek lawn on which the writers' community – Celia's phrase – was invited in summer to drink tea. At first Jane Dalgliesh had been excluded from the invitations, not because she didn't claim to be a writer but because she was a

solitary, elderly spinster and therefore, in Miss Calthrop's scale of values, a social and sexual failure rating only a patronising kindness. Then Miss Calthrop discovered that her neighbour was regarded as a distinguished woman by people well qualified to judge and that the men who, in defiance of propriety, were entertained at Pentlands and who were to be met trudging along the shore in happy companionship with their hostess were frequently themselves distinguished. A further discovery was more surprising. Jane Dalgliesh dined with R. B. Sinclair at Priory House. Not all those who praised Sinclair's three great novels, the last written over thirty years ago, realised that he was still alive. Fewer still were invited to dine with him. Miss Calthrop was not a woman obstinately to persist in error and Miss Dalgliesh became 'dear Jane' overnight. For her part she continued to call her neighbour 'Miss Calthrop' and was as unaware of the rapprochement as she had been of the original disdain. Dalgliesh was never sure what she really thought of Celia. She seldom spoke about her neighbours and the women were too rarely in each other's company for him to judge.

The rough track which led across Monksmere Head to Pentlands was less than fifty yards from Rosemary Cottage. It was usually barred by a heavy farm gate but today this stood open, biting deep into the tall hedge of brambles and elders. The car bumped slowly over the potholes and between the stubble of hay which soon gave way to grass and then to bracken. It passed the twin stone cottages belonging to Latham and Justin Bryce but Dalgliesh saw no sign of either man although Latham's Jaguar was parked at his door and there was a thin curl of smoke from Bryce's chimney. Now the track wound uphill and suddenly the whole of the headland lay open before him, stretching purple and golden to the cliffs and shining sea. At the crest of the track Dalgliesh stopped the car to watch and to listen. Autumn had never been his favourite season, but in the moment which followed the stopping of the engine he wouldn't have changed this mellow peace for all the keener sensitivities of spring. The heather was beginning to fade now

but the second flowering of the gorse was as thick and golden as the first richness of May. Beyond it lay the sea, streaked with purple, azure and brown, and to the south the mist-hung marshes of the bird reserve added their gentler greens and blues. The air smelt of heather and woodsmoke, the inevitable and evocative smells of autumn. It was hard to believe, thought Dalgliesh, that one was looking at a battlefield where for nearly nine centuries the land had waged its losing fight against the sea; hard to realise that under that deceptive calm of veined water lay the nine drowned churches of old Dunwich. There were few buildings standing on the headland now but not all were old. To the north Dalgliesh could just glimpse the low walls of Seton House, little more than an excrescence on the edge of the cliff, which Maurice Seton, the detective novelist, had built to suit his odd and solitary life. Half a mile to the south the great square walls of Priory House stood like a last bastion against the sea and, on the very edge of the bird reserve, Pentlands Cottage seemed to hang on the brink of nothingness. As his eyes scanned the headland a horse and buggy came into sight on the far north track and bowled merrily over the gorse towards Priory House. Dalgliesh could see a stout little body hunchbacked in the driving seat and the whip, delicate as a wand, erect by her side. It must be R. B. Sinclair's housekeeper bringing home the provisions. There was a charming domestic touch about the gay little equipage and Dalgliesh watched it with pleasure until it disappeared behind the shield of trees which half hid Priory House. At that moment his aunt appeared at the side of her cottage and gazed up the headland. Dalgliesh glanced at his wrist. It was thirty-three minutes past two. He let in the clutch and the Cooper Bristol bumped slowly down the track towards her.

CHAPTER THREE

Stepping back instinctively into the shadows of his upstairs room, Oliver Latham watched the car as it bounced gently up the headland and laughed aloud. Then he checked himself, silenced by the explosive sound of his laughter in the stillness of the cottage. But this was too much! Scotland Yard's wonder boy, still reeking from his latest blood sport, had come most promptly upon his cue. The car was stopping now on the crown of the headland. It would be pleasant if that damned Cooper Bristol had broken down at last. But no, it looked as if Dalgliesh was pausing simply to admire the view. The poor fool was probably relishing in advance the sweets of a fortnight's cosseting at Pentlands. Well, he was in for a surprise. The question was, would it be prudent for him, Latham, to stay around and watch the fun? Why not? He wasn't due back in town until the first night at the Court Theatre on Thursday week and it would look odd if he dashed back now so soon after his arrival. Besides, he was curious. He had driven to Monksmere on Wednesday expecting to be bored. But now, with luck, it was promising to be quite an exciting holiday.

CHAPTER FOUR

Alice Kerrison drove the buggy behind the fringe of trees which shielded Priory House from the northern part of the headland, bounced down from her seat and led the mare through the wide crumbling archway to a row of sixteenth-century stables. As she busied herself with the unharnessing, grunting a little with the effort, her practical mind complacently reviewed the morning's work and looked forward to the small domestic pleasures to come. First they would drink tea together, strong and over-sweet as Mr Sinclair liked it, sitting one each side of the great fire in the hall. Even on a warm

autumn day Mr Sinclair liked his fire. And then before the light began to fade and the mists rose, they would take their daily walk together across the headland. And it wouldn't be a walk without a purpose. There was some burying to be done. Well, it was always satisfactory to have an object and for all Mr Sinclair's clever talk, human remains however incomplete were still human remains and were entitled to respect. Besides, it was high time they were out of the house.

CHAPTER FIVE

It was nearly half-past eight and Dalgliesh and his aunt, their dinner over, sat in companionable silence one each side of the living room fire. The room, which occupied almost the whole of the ground floor of Pentlands, was stone walled with a low roof buttressed by immense oak beams and floor of red quarry tiles. In front of the open fireplace, where a wood fire crackled and spurted, a neat stack of driftwood was drying. The smell of wood smoke drifted through the cottage like incense; and the air vibrated endlessly with the thudding of the sea. Dalgliesh found it hard to keep awake in this rhythmic, somnambulant peace. He had always enjoyed contrast in art or nature and at Pentlands, once night had fallen, the pleasures of contrast were easily self-induced. Inside the cottage there was light and warmth, all the colours and comfort of civilised domesticity; outside under the low clouds there was darkness, solitude, mystery. He pictured the shore, one hundred feet below, where the sea was spreading its fringe of lace over the cold, firm beach; and the Monksmere bird reserve to the south, quiet under the night sky, its reeds hardly stirring in the still water.

Stretching his legs to the fire and wedging his head still more comfortably into the high back of the chair, he looked across at his aunt. She was sitting, as always, bolt upright and yet she looked perfectly comfortable. She was knitting a pair of wool-

len socks in bright red which Dalgliesh could only hope were not intended for him. He thought it unlikely. His aunt was not given to such domestic tokens of affection. The firelight threw gules on her long face, brown and carved as an Aztec's, the eyes hooded, the nose long and straight above a wide mobile mouth. Her hair was iron grey now, coiled into a huge bun in the nape of her neck. It was a face that he remembered from childhood. He had never seen any difference in her. Upstairs in her room, stuck casually into the edge of a looking glass, was the faded photograph of herself and her dead fiancé taken in 1916. Dalgliesh thought of it now; the boy, in the squashed peak cap and breeches which had once looked slightly ridiculous to him but now epitomised the romance and heartbreak of an age long dead; the girl half an inch taller, swaying towards him with the angular grace of adolescence, her hair dressed wide and ribbon bound, her feet in their pointed shoes just showing beneath the slim flowing skirt. Jane Dalgliesh had never talked to him of her youth and he had never asked. She was the most self-sufficient, the least sentimental woman that he knew. Dalgliesh wondered how Deborah would get on with her, what the two women would make of each other. It was difficult to picture Deborah in any setting other than London. Since her mother's death she hardly ever went home and, for reasons which they both understood only too well, he had never gone back to Martingale with her. He could only see her now against the background of his own City flat, of restaurants, theatre foyers and their favourite pubs. He was used to living his life on different levels. Deborah was not part of his job and as yet she had no place at Pentlands. But if he married her, she would necessarily have some share in both. Somehow, on this brief holiday he knew he had to decide if that was what he really wanted.

Jane Dalgliesh said:

'Would you like some music? I have the new Mahler recording.'

Dalgliesh wasn't musical, but he knew that music meant a

great deal to his aunt and listening to her records had become part of a Pentlands holiday. Her knowledge and pleasure were infectious; he was beginning to make discoveries. And, in his present mood, he was even ready to try Mahler.

It was then they heard the car.

'Oh, Lord,' he said. 'Who's this? Not Celia Calthrop, I hope.' Miss Calthrop, if not firmly discouraged, was an inveterate dropper in, trying always to impose on the solitariness of Monksmere the cosy conventions of suburban social life. She was particularly apt to call when Dalgliesh was at the cottage. To her a personable and unattached male was natural prey. If she didn't want him herself there was always somebody who did; she disliked seeing anything go to waste. On one of his visits she had actually given a cocktail party in his honour. At the time he had enjoyed it, intrigued by the essential incongruity of the occasion. The little group of Monksmere residents, meeting as if for the first time, had munched canapés and sipped cheap sherry in Celia's pink and white drawing room and made inconsequent polite conversation while, outside, a gale screamed across the headland and the sou'westers and storm lanterns were stacked in the hall. Here had been contrast indeed. But it was not a habit to encourage.

Jane Dalgliesh said:

'It sounds like Miss Calthrop's Morris. She may be bringing her niece. Elizabeth is home from Cambridge convalescing from glandular fever. I think she arrived yesterday.'

'Then she ought to be in bed. It sounds as if there are more than two of them. Isn't that Justin Bryce's bleat?'

It was. When Miss Dalgliesh opened the door they could see through the porch windows the twin lights of the car and a confusion of dark forms which gradually resolved themselves into familiar figures. It looked as if the whole of Monksmere was calling on his aunt. Even Sylvia Kedge, Maurice Seton's crippled secretary, was with them, creeping on her crutches towards the stream of light from the open door. Miss Calthrop walked slowly beside her as if in support. Behind them was

Justin Bryce, still bleating inconsequently into the night. The tall figure of Oliver Latham loomed up beside him. Last of all, sulky and reluctant, came Elizabeth Marley, shoulders hunched, hands dug into her jacket pockets. She was loitering on the path and peering from side to side into the darkness as if dissociating herself from the party. Bryce called:

'Good evening, Miss Dalgliesh. Good evening, Adam. Don't blame me for this invasion. It's all Celia's idea. We've come for professional advice, my dears. All except Oliver. We met him on the way and he's only come to borrow some coffee. Or so he says.'

Latham said calmly:

'I forgot to buy coffee when I was driving from town yesterday. So I decided to call on my one neighbour who could be trusted to provide a decent blend without an accompanying lecture on my inefficient housekeeping. If I'd known you were having a party I might have waited until tomorrow.'

But he showed no inclination to go.

They came in, blinking in the light and bringing with them a gust of cold air which billowed the white wood smoke across the room. Celia Calthrop went straight to Dalgliesh's chair and arranged herself as if to receive an evening's homage. Her elegant legs and feet, carefully displayed to advantage, were in marked contrast to her heavy, stoutly-corseted body with its high bosom, and her flabby mottled arms. Dalgliesh supposed that she must be in her late forties but she looked older. As always she was heavily but skilfully made up. The little vulpine mouth was carmine, the deep-set and downward sloping eyes which gave her face a look of spurious spirituality much emphasised in her publicity photographs were blue shadowed, he lashes weighted with mascara. She took off her chiffon headscarf to reveal her hairdresser's latest effort, the hair fine as a baby's through which the glimpses of pink, smooth scalp looked almost indecent.

Dalgliesh had only met her niece twice before and now, shaking hands, he thought that Cambridge had not changed

her. She was still the sulky, heavy-featured girl that he remembered. It was not an unintelligent face and might even have been attractive if only it had held a spark of animation.

The room had lost its peace. Dalgliesh reflected that it was extraordinary how much noise seven people could make. There was the usual business of settling Sylvia Kedge into her chair which Miss Calthrop supervised imperiously, although she did nothing active to help. The girl would have been called unusual, perhaps even beautiful, if only one could have forgotten those twisted ugly legs, braced into calipers, the heavy shoulders, the masculine hands distorted by her crutches. Her face was long, brown as a gypsy's and framed by shoulder-length black hair brushed straight from a centre parting. It was a face which could have held strength and character but she had imposed on it a look of piteous humility, an air of suffering, meekly and uncomplainingly borne, which sat incongruously on that high brow. The great black eyes were skilled in inviting compassion. She was now adding to the general fluster by asserting that she was perfectly comfortable when she obviously wasn't, suggesting with a deprecating gentleness which had all the force of a command that her crutches should be placed within reach even though this meant propping them insecurely against her knees, and by generally making all present uncomfortably aware of their own undeserved good health. Dalgliesh had watched this play-acting before, but tonight he sensed that her heart wasn't in it, that the routine was almost mechanical. For once the girl looked genuinely ill and in pain. Her eyes were as dull as stones and there were lines running deeply between her nostrils and the corners of her mouth. She looked as if she needed sleep, and when he gave her a glass of sherry he saw that her hand was trembling. Seized by a spasm of genuine compassion, he wrapped his fingers around hers and steadied the glass until she could drink. Smiling at her he asked gently:

'Well, what's the trouble? What can I do to help?'

But Celia Calthrop had appointed herself spokesman.

'It's too bad of us all to come worrying you and Jane on your first evening together. I do realise that. But we're very worried. At least, Sylvia and I are. Deeply concerned.'

'While I,' said Justin Bryce, 'am not so much worried as intrigued, not to say hopeful. Maurice Seton's disappeared. I'm afraid it may only be a publicity stunt for his next thriller and that we shall see him among us again all too soon. But let us not look on the gloomy side.'

He did, indeed, look very far from gloomy, squatting on a stool before the fire like a malevolent turtle, twisting his long neck towards the blaze. His had been, in youth, a striking head with its high cheekbones, wide mobile lips and huge luminous grey eyes under the heavy lids. But he was fifty now and becoming a caricature. Though they seemed even larger, his eyes were less bright, and watered perpetually as if he were always fighting against a high wind. The receding hair had faded and coarsened to dull straw. The bones jutted through his skin giving him the appearance of a death's head. Only his hands were unchanged. He held them out now to the fire, soft-skinned, white and delicate as those of a girl. He smiled at Dalgliesh:

'Lost, believed safe. One middle-aged detective writer. Nervous disposition. Slight build. Narrow nose. Buck teeth. Sparse hair. Prominent Adam's apple. Finder, please keep . . . So we come to you for advice, dear boy. Fresh, as I understand it, from your latest triumph. Do we wait for Maurice to make his reappearance and then pretend we didn't notice that he got lost? Or do we play it his way and ask the police to help us find him? After all, if it is a publicity stunt, it would only be kind to co-operate. Poor Maurice needs all the help in that direction he can get.'

'It's not a joking matter, Justin.' Miss Calthrop was severe. 'And I don't for one moment think that it's a publicity stunt. If I did, I wouldn't come worrying Adam at a time when he particularly needs a peaceful, quiet holiday to recover from the strain of that case. So clever of you, Adam, to catch him before

19

he did it again. The whole case makes me feel sick, physically sick! And now what will happen to him? Kept in prison for a few years at the State's expense, then let out to murder some other child? Are we all mad in this country? I can't think why we don't hang him mercifully and be done with it.'

Dalgliesh was glad that his face was in shadow. He recalled again the moment of arrest. Pooley had been such a small man, small, ugly and stinking with fear. His wife had left him a year before and the inexpert patch which puckered the elbow of his cheap suit had obviously been his own work. Dalgliesh had found his eyes held by that patch as if it had the power to assert that Pooley was still a human being. Well, the beast was caged now and the public and press were free to be loud in their praise of the police work in general and of Superintendent Dalgliesh in particular. A psychiatrist could explain, no doubt, why he felt himself contaminated with guilt. The feeling was not new to him and he would deal with it in his own way. After all, he reflected wryly, it had seldom inconvenienced him for long and never once had it made him want to change his job. But he was damned if he was going to discuss Pooley with Celia Calthrop.

Across the room his aunt's eyes met his. She said quietly:

'What exactly do you want my nephew to do, Miss Calthrop? If Mr Seton has disappeared, isn't that a matter for the local police?'

'But is it? That's our problem!' Miss Calthrop drained her glass as if the Amontillado had been cooking sherry, and automatically held it out to be refilled.

'Maurice may have disappeared for some purpose of his own, perhaps to collect material for his next book. He's been hinting that this is to be something different – a departure from his usual classical detective novel. He's a most conscientious craftsman and doesn't like to deal with anything outside his personal experience. We all know that. Remember how he spent three months with a travelling circus before he wrote *Murder on the High Wire*? Of course, it does imply he's a little

deficient in creative imagination. My novels are never restricted to my own experience.'

Justin Bryce said:

'In view of what your last heroine went through, Celia darling, I'm relieved to hear it.'

Dalgliesh asked when Seton had last been seen. Before Miss Calthrop could answer, Sylvia Kedge spoke. The sherry and the warmth of the fire had put some colour into her cheeks and she had herself well under control. She spoke directly to Dalgliesh and without interruption.

'Mr Seton went to London last Monday morning to stay at his Club, that's the Cadaver Club in Tavistock Square. He always spends a week or two there in October. He prefers London in the autumn and he likes to do research for his books in the Club Library. He took a small suitcase with him and his portable typewriter. He went by the train from Halesworth. He told me that he was going to make a start on a new book, something different from his usual style, and I got the impression he was rather excited about it although he never discussed it with me. He said that everyone would be surprised by it. He arranged for me to work at the house for mornings only while he was away and said he would telephone me about ten o'clock if he had any messages. That's the usual arrangement when he's working at the Club. He types the manuscript in double spacing and posts it to me in instalments and I make a fair copy. Then he revises the whole book and I type it ready for the publishers. Of course, the instalments don't always connect. When he's in London he likes to work on town scenes – I never know what's going to arrive next. Well, he telephoned on Tuesday morning to say that he hoped to post some manuscript by Wednesday evening and to ask me to do one or two small mending jobs. He sounded perfectly all right, perfectly normal then.'

Miss Calthrop could contain herself no longer.

'It was really very naughty of Maurice to use you for jobs like darning his socks and polishing the silver. You're a

qualified shorthand typist and it's a dreadful waste of skill. Goodness knows, I've enough stuff on tape waiting for you to type. However, that's another matter. Everyone knows my views.'

Everyone did. There would have been more sympathy with them if people hadn't suspected that dear Celia's indignation was chiefly on her own account. If there was any exploiting to be done she expected priority.

The girl took no notice of her interruption. Her dark eyes were still fixed on Dalgliesh. He asked gently:

'When did you next hear from Mr Seton?'

'I didn't, Mr Dalgliesh. There was no call on Wednesday when I was working at Seton House but, of course, that didn't worry me. He might not telephone for days. I was there again early this morning to finish some ironing when Mr Plant rang. He's the caretaker at the Cadaver Club and his wife does the cooking. He said they were very worried because Mr Seton had gone out before dinner on Tuesday and hadn't returned to the Club. His bed hadn't been slept in and his clothes and type-writer were still there. Mr Plant didn't like to make too much fuss at first. He thought that Mr Seton might have stayed out for some purpose connected with his work – but he got worried when a second night went by and still no message. So he thought he'd better telephone the house. I didn't know what to do. I couldn't contact Mr Seton's half-brother because he recently moved to a new flat and we don't know the address. There aren't any other relations. You see, I wasn't sure whether Mr Seton would want me to take any action. I suggested to Mr Plant that we should wait a little longer and we agreed to phone each other the minute there was any news, and then just before lunch time, the post arrived and I got the manuscript.'

'We have it here,' proclaimed Miss Calthrop. 'And the envelope.' She produced them from her capacious handbag with a flourish and handed them to Dalgliesh. The envelope was the ordinary commercial, buff-coloured, four-by-nine-inch size and was addressed, in typing, to Maurice Seton, Esq., Seton

House, Monksmere, Suffolk. Inside were three quarto sheets of inexpert typescript, double spaced. Miss Kedge said dully:

'He always addressed the manuscript to himself. But that isn't his work, Mr Dalgliesh. He didn't write it and he didn't type it.'

'How can you be sure?'

It was hardly a necessary question. There are few things more difficult to disguise than typing and the girl had surely copied enough Maurice Seton manuscripts to recognise his style. But before she had a chance to reply, Miss Calthrop said:

'I think it would be best if I just read part of it.'

They waited while she took from her handbag a pair of immense jewelled spectacles, settled them on her nose, and arranged herself more comfortably in the chair. Maurice Seton, thought Dalgliesh, was about to have his first public reading. He would have been gratified by the listeners' rapt attention and possibly, too, by Miss Calthrop's histrionics. Celia, faced with the work of a fellow craftsman and sure of the audience, was prepared to give of her best. She read:

'Carruthers pushed aside the bead curtain and entered the night club. For a moment he stood motionless in the doorway, his tall figure elegant as always in the well-cut dinner jacket, his cool ironic eyes surveying with a kind of disdain the close-packed tables, the squalid pseudo-Spanish decor, the shabby clientèle. So this was the headquarters of perhaps the most dangerous gang in Europe! Behind this sordid but common-place night club, outwardly no different from a hundred others in Soho, was a master mind which could control some of the most powerful criminal gangs in the West. It seemed unlikely. But then, this whole fantastic adventure was unlikely. He sat down at the table nearest the door to watch and wait. When the waiter came he ordered fried scampi, green salad and a bottle of Chianti. The man, a grubby little Cypriot, took his order without a word. Did they know he was here, Carruthers wondered. And, if they did, how long would it be before they showed themselves?

'There was a small stage at the end of the Club furnished only with a cane screen and a single red chair. Suddenly the lights were dimmed and the pianist began to play a slow sensuous tune. From behind the screen came a girl. She was blonde and beautiful, not young but mature and full bosomed, with a grace and arrogance which Carruthers thought might indicate White Russian blood. She moved forward sensuously to the single chair and with great deliberation began to unzip her evening dress. It fell about her knees to the ground. Underneath she wore nothing but a black brassière and G string. Sitting now with her back to the audience she twisted her hands to unhook the brassière. Immediately from the crowded tables there came a hoarse murmuring. "Rosie! Rosie! Come on, Rosie! Give! Give!"'

Miss Calthrop stopped reading. There was complete silence. Most of her listeners seemed stunned. Then Bryce called out:

'Well, go on, Celia! Don't stop now it's getting really exciting. Does Rosie fall on the Hon. Martin Carruthers and rape him? He's had it coming to him for years. Or is that too much to hope?'

Miss Calthrop said:

'There's no need to go on. The proof we need is there.'

Sylvia Kedge turned again to Dalgliesh.

'Mr Seton would never call a character Rosie, Mr Dalgliesh. That was his mother's name. He told me once that he would never use it in any of his books. And he never did.'

'Particularly not for a Soho prostitute,' broke in Miss Calthrop. 'He talked to me about his mother quite often. He adored her. Absolutely adored her. It nearly broke his heart when she died and his father married again.'

Miss Calthrop's voice throbbed with all the yearning of frustrated motherhood. Suddenly Oliver Latham said:

'Let me see that.'

Celia handed the manuscript to him and they all watched with anxious expectancy while he scanned it. Then he handed it back without a word.

'Well?' asked Miss Calthrop.

'Nothing. I just wanted to have a look at it. I know Seton's handwriting but not his typing. But you say that he didn't type this.'

'I'm sure he didn't,' said Miss Kedge. 'Although I can't exactly say why. It just doesn't look like his work. But it was typed on his machine.'

'What about the style?' asked Dalgliesh. The little group considered. At last Bryce said:

'One couldn't really call that typical Seton. After all, the man could write when he chose. It's almost artificial, isn't it? One gets the impression he was trying to write badly.'

Elizabeth Marley had been silent until now, sitting alone in the corner like a discontented child who has been dragged unwillingly into the company of boring adults. Suddenly she said impatiently:

'If this is a fake it's obvious we were meant to discover it. Justin's right. The style's completely bogus. And it's too much of a coincidence that the person responsible should have hit on the one name which would arouse suspicion. Why choose Rosie? If you ask me, this is just Maurice Seton trying to be clever and you've all fallen for it. You'll read all about it when his new book comes out. You know how he loves experimenting.'

'It's certainly the sort of childish scheme that Seton might think up,' said Latham. 'I'm not sure I want to be an involuntary participant in any of his damn silly experiments. I suggest we forget the whole thing. He'll turn up in his own time.'

'Maurice was always very odd and secretive, of course,' agreed Miss Calthrop. 'Especially about his work. And there's another thing. I've been able to give him one or two useful little hints in the past. He's definitely used them. But never a word to me subsequently. Naturally I didn't expect a formal acknowledgement. If I can help a fellow writer I'm only too happy. But it's a little disconcerting when a book is published

to find one or two of one's own ideas in the plot and never a thank you from Maurice.'

'He's probably forgotten by then that he didn't think them out for himself,' suggested Latham with a kind of tolerant contempt.

'He never forgot anything, Oliver. Maurice had a very clear mind. He worked methodically too. If I dropped a suggestion he'd pretend to be only half interested and mutter something about trying to work it in sometime or other. But I could see from the look in his eyes that he'd seized on it and was only waiting to get home to file it away on one of those little index cards. Not that I resented it really. It's just that I think he might have acknowledged the help occasionally. I gave him an idea a month or so ago and I bet you anything it will appear in the next book.'

No one accepted the offer. Bryce said:

'You're absolutely right about him, Celia. One contributed one's own mite from time to time. God knows why except that one does get the occasional idea for a new method of murder and it seemed a shame to waste it when poor Seton was so obviously near the end of his resources. But, apart from that predatory gleam in his eye – not a sign of appreciation, my dears! Of course, for reasons you all appreciate, he gets no help from me now. Not after what he did to Arabella.'

Miss Calthrop said:

'Oh, my idea wasn't for a new method of murder exactly. It was just a situation. I thought it might make rather an effective opening chapter. I kept telling Maurice that you must capture your readers from the very start. I pictured a body drifting out to sea in a dinghy with its hands chopped off at the wrists.'

There was a silence, so complete, so sudden that the striking of the carriage clock drew all their eyes towards it as if it were chiming the hour of execution. Dalgliesh was looking at Latham. He had stiffened in his chair and was grasping the stem of his glass with such force that Dalgliesh half expected it to snap. It was impossible to guess what lay behind that pale,

rigid mask. Suddenly Bryce gave his high, nervous laugh and the tension broke. One could almost hear the little gasps of relief.

'What an extraordinarily morbid imagination you have, Celia! One would never suspect. You must control these impulses, my dear, or the League of Romantic Novelists will hurl you out of the Club.'

Latham spoke, his voice controlled, colourless. He said:

'All this doesn't help with the present problem. Do I take it that we're agreed to take no action about Seton's disappearance? Eliza is probably right and it's just some nonsense Maurice has thought up. If so the sooner we leave Mr Dalgliesh to enjoy his holiday in peace the better.'

He was rising to go as if suddenly wearied of the whole subject when there was a loud authoritative knock on the cottage door. Jane Dalgliesh lifted an interrogative eyebrow at her nephew then got up silently and went through the porch to open it. The party fell silent, listening unashamedly. A caller after dusk was rare in their isolated community. Once night fell they were used to seeing only each other and knew by instinct of long experience whose footstep was approaching their door. But this loud summons had been the knock of a stranger. There was the soft, broken mutter of voices from the porch. Then Miss Dalgliesh reappeared in the doorway, two raincoated men in the shadows behind her. She said:

'This is Detective Inspector Reckless and Sergeant Courtney from the County CID. They are looking for Digby Seton. His sailing dinghy has come ashore at Cod Head.'

Justin Bryce said:

'That's odd. It was beached as usual at the bottom of Tanner's Lane at five o'clock yesterday afternoon.'

Everyone seemed to realise simultaneously how strange it was that a Detective Inspector and a Sergeant should be calling after dark about a missing dinghy but Latham spoke before the others had formed their questions:

'What's wrong, Inspector?'

Jane Dalgliesh replied for him.

'Something very shocking, I'm afraid. Maurice Seton's body was in the boat.'

'Maurice's body! Maurice? But that's ridiculous!' Miss Calthrop's sharp didactic voice cut across the room in futile protest.

'It can't be Maurice. He never takes the boat out. Maurice doesn't like sailing.'

The Inspector moved forward into the light and spoke for the first time.

'He hadn't been sailing, Madam. Mr Seton was lying dead in the bottom of the boat. Dead, and with both hands taken off at the wrists.'

CHAPTER SIX

Celia Calthrop, as if relishing her own obstinacy, said for the tenth time:

'I keep telling you! I didn't say a word about the plot to anyone except Maurice. Why should I? And it's no good harping on about the date. It was about six months ago – perhaps longer. I can't remember just when. But we were walking along the beach to Walberswick and I suddenly thought that it would make a good start to a detective story if one described a handless corpse drifting out to sea in a boat. So I suggested it to Maurice. I certainly never mentioned it to anyone else until tonight. Maurice may have done so, of course.'

Elizabeth Marley burst out irritably:

'Obviously he told someone! We can hardly suppose that he cut his own hands off in the cause of verisimilitude. And it's stretching coincidence too far to suggest that you and the murderer happened to think of the same idea. But I don't see how you can be so certain that you didn't talk about it to anyone else. I believe you mentioned it to me once when we were discussing how slow Maurice was to get his plots under way.'

28

No one looked as if they believed her. Justin Bryce said softly, but not so softly that the others couldn't hear:

'Dear Eliza! So loyal always.' Oliver Latham laughed and there was a short, embarrassed silence broken by Sylvia Kedge's hoarse belligerent voice.

'He never mentioned it to me.'

'No dear,' replied Miss Calthrop sweetly. 'But then, there were a great many things which Mr Seton didn't discuss with you. One doesn't tell everything to one's maid. And that, my dear, was how he thought of you. You should have had more pride than to let him use you as a household drudge. Men prefer a little spirit, you know.'

It was gratuitously spiteful and Dalgliesh could sense the general embarrassed surprise. But no one spoke. He was almost ashamed to look at the girl but she had bent her head as if meekly accepting a merited rebuke, and the two black swathes of hair had swung forward to curtain her face. In the sudden silence he could hear the rasping of her breath, and he wished he could feel sorry for her. Certainly Celia Calthrop was intolerable; but there was something about Sylvia Kedge which provoked unkindness. He wondered what lay behind that particular impulse to savagery.

It was nearly an hour since Inspector Reckless and his Sergeant had arrived, an hour in which the Inspector had said little and the rest of the company, except Dalgliesh and his aunt, had said a great deal. Not all of it had been wise. Reckless had settled himself on arrival in a high chair against the wall and sat there still, solid as a bailiff, his sombre eyes watchful in the light of the fire. Despite the warmth of the room he was wearing his raincoat, a grubby gaberdine which looked too fragile to sustain the weight of its armour of metal buttons, buckles and studs. On his lap he nursed with careful hands a pair of immense gauntlet gloves and a trilby hat as if fearful that someone was going to snatch them from him. He looked like an interloper; the minor official there on sufferance, the little man who dares not risk a drink on duty. And that,

thought Dalgliesh, was exactly the effect he aimed to produce. Like all successful detectives, he was able to subdue his personality at will so that even his physical presence became as innocuous and commonplace as a piece of furniture. The man was helped by his appearance, of course. He was small – surely only just the regulation height for a policeman – and the sallow, anxious face was as neutral and unremarkable as any of a million faces seen crowding into a football ground on a Saturday afternoon. His voice, too, was flat, classless, giving no clue to the man. His eyes, wide spaced and deep set under jutting brows, had a trick of moving expressionlessly from face to face as people spoke, which the present company might have found disconcerting if they had bothered to notice. By his side, Sergeant Courtney sat with the air of one who has been told to sit upright, keep his eyes and ears open and say nothing, and who is doing just that.

Dalgliesh glanced across the room to where his aunt sat in her usual chair, she had taken up her knitting and seemed serenely detached from the business in hand. She had been taught to knit by a German governess and held the needles upright in the Continental manner; Celia Calthrop seemed mesmerised by their flashing tips and sat glaring across at them as if both fascinated and affronted by her hostess's unusual expertise. She was less at ease, crossing and uncrossing her feet and jerking back her head from the fire as if she found its heat intolerable. It was certainly getting hot in the sitting room. All the other visitors, except Reckless, seemed to feel it too. Oliver Latham was pacing up and down, his brow wet with sweat, his restless energy seeming to raise the temperature still higher. Suddenly he swung round at Reckless:

'When did he die?' he demanded. 'Come on, let's have some facts for a change! When did Seton die?'

'We shan't know that precisely until we get the PM report, Sir.'

'In other words, you're not telling. Let me phrase it another way then. For what hours are we expected to provide alibis?'